This Bing book belongs to:

....

Copyright © 2020 Acamar Films Ltd

The *Bing* television series is created by Acamar Films and Brown Bag Films
and adapted from the original books by Ted Dewan

Original story written by Denise Cassar, Mikael Shields and Claire Jennings

Bing's Snowy Day was adapted from the original television script by Rebecca Gerlings

First published in the UK in 2020 by HarperCollins *Children's Books*
A division of HarperCollins Publishers Ltd, 1 London Bridge Street, London SE1 9GF

1 3 5 7 9 10 8 6 4 2

ISBN: 978-0-00-838212-4

Printed in China

MIX
Paper from
responsible sources
FSC® C007454

FSC
www.fsc.org

FSC is a non-profit international organisation established to promote the
responsible management of the world's forests. Products carrying the FSC
label are independently certified to assure consumers that they come
from forests that are managed to meet the social, economic and
ecological needs of present and future generations.

Find out more about HarperCollins and the environment at
www.harpercollins.co.uk/green

Bing's Snowy Day

HarperCollins *Children's Books*

Round the corner, not far away,
it's **snowing** today!

Bing, Sula and her little cousin, Nicky, are at Bing's house watching the **snowflakes** fall outside.

"Snoooooow!" gasps Nicky.

"Yay!" cries Bing excitedly. "I can *voosh* in my new Hoppity Rocket Sledge!"

Before they go outside, Amma and Flop help Bing, Sula and Nicky wrap up warm and toasty.

Flop helps Bing put on his gloves. "If you don't wear them, the snow will give you ouchy hands."

But Bing is so excited to play in the snow that he forgets to listen.

Out in the garden, Bing can't wait to get

voooshing!

"Sula, can you pull **me first?**" he calls from his shiny new Hoppity Rocket Sledge.

"OK!" Sula agrees, tugging the rope.

"Nicky sledge!" calls Nicky. He wants a turn too.

But keeping the sledge moving
in the garden is hard work.

"Urgh! I *can't* pull any more!" puffs Sula.

"You need a hill, Bing!" explains Amma.

Bing tests the sledge out. Amma's right – it just isn't very *vooshy* without a hill to slide down.

Then Sula has a
good idea . . .

"Bing, come
and build a
snowman
with us!"

"OK!" says Bing. "I can do **Mr Snowman's head!**"
He takes off his gloves and begins to roll a snowball.

When it's big enough, Bing pushes his snowball
into place on top of Sula and Nicky's snow pile.

"Yay!" they all shout.

"We did it, Bing!" says Sula.

Bing grins proudly. "Hello, Mr Snowman!"

"Oh!" exclaims Amma. "He's going to be a *lovely* snowman. But I think he needs a face . . ."

"I'll go and see if I can find a carrot,"
says Flop, heading inside.

"And we need stones!" Bing tells Sula and Nicky.

He digs his hands deep down in the snow,
searching for stones to make eyes and a mouth.

"Oh! Found one."

Bing finds the **perfect stone** to complete the snowman's smile.

"This could be for his mouth," says Bing, patting it on the **snowman**.

"Oh, that's lovely, Bing!" says Sula.

Flop returns with a carrot. Bing pushes it into the snowman's face, but afterwards he notices his hands feel *really* ouchy . . .

"Oh . . . oh . . . oh . . . OWWW!" he cries.

"Come on inside, Bing," says Flop. "Let's warm your hands up."

Inside, Flop gives Bing's hands a rub to help them warm up.

"If they get cold in the snow, they feel ouchy until you warm them up again," explains Flop. "It just takes a bit of time."

Amma has an idea to help Bing forget about his ouchy hands. "Here, Bing. Help me decorate the lanterns for the Christmas parade!"

"Hmmm, this can go here," says Bing, sticking on a shiny paper star.

"Oh, *yes* – I like that!" admires Flop
when Bing's starry lantern is finished.

"Sula! Nicky!" Amma calls outside. "It's time
to get ready for our Christmas parade!"

But Bing doesn't want to go outside. He's afraid his hands will **get all ouchy** again.

"It'll be all right," Amma says, "if you **wear your gloves.**"

"My hands didn't get OUCHY, Bing," says Sula, showing him her sparkly gloves.

Nicky holds out his gloved hands too.
"Bing glove!"

"I thought we could take your Hoppity Rocket Sledge to the park and *voosh* down Windy Hill," Flop suggests.

"Oh! *Can* I, Flop?" exclaims Bing excitedly. "And I can put my gloves on!"

"Indeed," replies Flop with a chuckle.

Bing leads the way, pulling his
Hoppity Rocket Sledge behind him.

"Let's go-go-go-go-go!"

When they get to Windy Hill, it's dusk and fresh
snow is falling. Everything looks magical.

Bing climbs into his Hoppity Rocket Sledge, and . . .

... **VOOSH!**

"Look, Flop!
I'm **VOOOOOshing!**"
Bing shouts as he slides
down the snowy slope
towards his friends.

"Good for you, Bing!" Flop says
when Bing reaches the bottom.

Nicky wants a go in the Hoppity Rocket Sledge too.
"*Voosh* Nicky!" he says, giggling.

"Yes, Nicky, you can *voosh* now too!" says Bing.
Everybody loves the Hoppity Rocket Sledge!

**Playing in the snow . . .
it's a Bing thing.**